The Best Worst Brother

Stephanie Stuve-Bodeen
Illustrations by Charlotte Fremaux

Woodbine House   2005

Text © 2005 Stephanie Stuve-Bodeen
Illustrations © Charlotte Murray Fremaux

All rights reserved. Published in the United States of America by Woodbine House Inc.,
6510 Bells Mill Rd., Bethesda, MD 20817. 800-843-7323. *www.woodbinehouse.com*

Library of Congress Cataloging-in-Publication Data

Stuve-Bodeen, Stephanie, 1965-
    The best worst brother / written by Stephanie Stuve-Bodeen ; illustrated by Charlotte Murray Fremaux.—
1st ed.
            p. cm.
    Summary: Older sister Emma tries to be patient while teaching three-year-old Isaac, who has Down syn-
drome, how to communicate using sign language. Includes questions and answers about sign language.
    ISBN 1-890627-68-2
    [1. Brothers and sisters—Fiction. 2. Down syndrome—Fiction. 3. Sign language—Fiction.]
    I. Fremaux, Charlotte Murray, ill. II. Title.
    PZ7+
    [E]—dc22
                                                                                            2005000272

Manufactured in China

First edition
10   9   8   7   6   5   4   3   2   1

For Mitch, Cheryl, Roger, Martyne, and Steven:
Grandma Stuve would be so proud of our families.

And for Kate and Jess: Grandma Tiny would also be extremely proud.
(But Seth would still get more presents.)

My brother Isaac is not like other little brothers. He is *worse*.

I liked him better when he was just a baby. I held him and he just sat there, looking up at me, smelling like baby shampoo and making sweet baby sounds.

Now he's almost three, and when I try to hold him, he just kicks and screeches and wants to get down.

When Isaac was a baby, I helped my mom feed him smashed bananas. I made sounds like an airplane and flew the spoon into his mouth when he opened up.

Now, he sits in his
highchair and spits out
his food and throws it
all over.
    Yuck!

When Isaac was a baby, all I had to do was run around and act goofy and make silly faces and he'd laugh until he got hiccups.

Now, nothing I do makes him happy.

He loves to play blocks, and I
try to play too, but he wants
them all to himself.
If I ever do build
something, he just
knocks it down.

My dad said Isaac will be fun to play with again someday, but I'm tired of waiting. I think he acts mean because he can't talk yet. So, I'm trying to teach him how.

My mom said it will be easier for Isaac to use his hands to make words instead of his voice. She is taking a class in sign language and is teaching me some signs.

When I play blocks with Isaac, I hold one up and make the sign for "please." I say, "Please! Can you say please, Isaac?"
He never does.

I give him the block anyway, and make the sign for "thank you." I say, "Thank you! Can you say thank you, Isaac?"
He never does.

Last night I held up a block. I made the sign for "please" and said, "Please!" Isaac grabbed the block.

I made the sign for "thank you" and said, "Thank you!"

Isaac spit at me and pushed me away.

I stood and yelled, "I give up!" Then I stomped up to my room.

My dad came later to tuck me in.

"Emma, you can't get so mad at Isaac."

"He'll never learn to talk!" I said.

"Remember when Isaac was born, and we talked about all the things he would do someday?"

I nodded.

"What did we agree to do?"

"Be patient."

"Exactly," said my dad, kissing my forehead. "He'll learn to talk when he's ready."

"I don't want to
wait," I said.
My dad smiled as
he turned out the light.
"Big sisters never do."

Today was Open House at my classroom. My mom and dad came with Isaac. Some of the other kids had younger brothers or sisters too. But they could talk. I was afraid someone might ask why Isaac couldn't.

Miss Becker came over to my family. She held a plate of cookies and Isaac tried to grab some from her. I felt my face turn red. But Miss Becker just smiled and said to Isaac, "You must be hungry!"

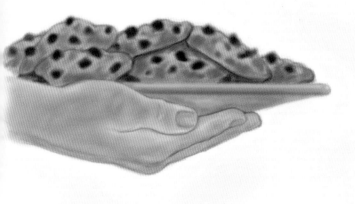

"Wait!" I said. "Look at Isaac!"
Isaac was holding his hand on his
chest, trying to move it in a circle.
    "Please! He's trying to say please!"
I helped him get it right.

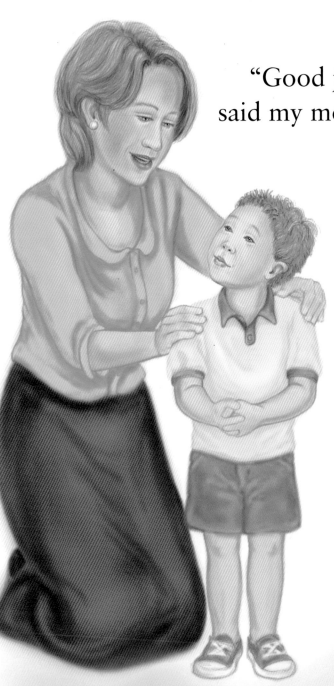

"Good job, Isaac!"
said my mom.

Good job,
Emma!" said
my dad.

Miss Becker gave Isaac
a cookie and he took a
bite. But then he put his
hand on his chin.

I jumped up and down.
"He's saying thank you!"

Then, of course, Isaac threw the rest of the cookie and hit Miss Becker in the head.

My mom and dad turned red, but Miss Becker just laughed. "That is just what my little brother would have done at that age."

I wondered. Isaac? Like other
little brothers?
No way! He's *better*.

Questions & Answers about Sign Language

What is sign language?

Sign language is a way to "talk" without speaking. Instead of using your mouth to make words, you use your fingers and hands and sometimes your face. In sign language, each word is formed with a special hand shape or movement. People who use sign language can say all the same things that people who speak can say—they just use words you see instead of words you hear.

Who uses sign language?

Lots of people! Sign language is most often used by people who have trouble hearing or who can't hear at all. But it is also used by some people who have trouble saying words clearly enough for others to understand. Many people think it's a good idea to teach sign language to *all* babies before they learn to speak so they can get their messages across as soon as possible.

Why do so many kids with Down syndrome use sign language?

Talking can be very hard for babies and children with Down syndrome. One big reason is that they often have weak muscles or problems getting their muscles to work together right. This includes the muscles in the tongue, lips, and mouth that are used to make speech sounds. It is not that they don't have anything to say. It is that they can't get their mouth muscles to say what they want. So, sign language helps them express themselves with their hands until they can say the words with their mouths. And they don't get so frustrated because now other people can tell what they want.

If a child with Down syndrome learns to use sign language, does that mean he will never talk?

No. Most kids with Down syndrome learn to talk by about age three or four (sometimes later). Using sign language does not keep them from learning to talk. People who use signs with them usually say the words at the same time they are making the signs. They also encourage them to say the parts of words they *can* say—like "ba" for ball or bath. Most children with Down syndrome just naturally stop using signs when they can say the words instead.

Is there such a thing as "baby talk" in sign language?

Yes. You know how some babies say things like "ba-ba" instead of "bottle" or "kee" instead of "kitty"? They usually do this because the real word is too hard for them to say. Well, if a sign is too hard for a baby or young child to make, she will also make the sign simpler. For example, when a baby signs "more," she might clap her hands instead of putting all her fingertips together. To a baby, this looks about the same and it's much easier to do.

Can I learn sign language?

Yes. If your parents are teaching your brother or sister sign language, you can learn it at the same time. Just ask to join in! Your brother or sister will be very excited.

Can I teach my brother or sister to use sign language like Emma did?

Probably. Ask your mom or dad how you can help. They most likely want to start with just a few important words, like Emma's parents did. You can make a sign and say the word for it, being sure your brother or sister is watching what you are doing. But be patient! Little kids need to see a sign many times before they are able to make it themselves. Remember, your brother or sister's first signs might not look so perfect at first. But give him lots of encouragement so he'll keep trying.

What should I say if I meet someone who uses sign language?

That depends. If the person can hear you speak or can read your lips, you can probably talk to her just as you would to anyone else. Slow down and talk more clearly if she has trouble understanding you. If you know some signs yourself, you can try signing and speaking the words at the same time. If you don't know sign language, it's always nice to smile, look the person in the eyes, and say "Hi" with a wave. Everyone understands this sign!

Special thanks to Libby Kumin, Ph.D., CCC-SLP,
for reviewing these questions and answers for accuracy.